Plexi & Flexi

In Adventures Around the Universe

Khalia Spear

Children Write Books Publications
 a Division of Nuvo Development, Inc.
Created by Patricia Dixon (*aka Ra Heter Ku-t*)
& Timothy Spear (*aka Mu Skher Aahku*)

P.O. Box 373015
Decatur, GA 30037

ISBN: 978-0-9719004-1-7

Written by Khalia Spear
Illustrated by Sakshi Mangal

Once upon a time a team of six heroes went on a mission to save the universe from being destroyed by villains. They go to places you have never seen or heard of before, like Metrodone and Zolar, with ancient mysteries and Black Holes.

They have a lot of powers that you would never imagine! They have
force. They are able to make things in record time.

Plexi is a genius. She has the biggest brain in the universe. Flexi is Plexi's twin sister. I know what you're thinking, they sound like aliens. Well they are aliens. Isn't that great!

Flexi is a super stretching woman. She is like a gymnast, but with more stretch.

The next member of the team is Wonder Girl. She is the daughter of Wonder Lady. Wonder Girl has six to seven powers. Some of them are cool and some are not.

Aqua Blue is a man who shoots water. He can also transform into water. Isn't that an awesome thing to be able to do!

Stan Stillman is very strong and can actually freeze anything he touches. That's why he wears gloves all the time.

Mechanical Med is a mechanic. He isn't just any mechanic; he can build anything in two seconds flat. He is very useful for a lot of missions.

They were all on planet Metradone, when all of sudden...BOOM! "What was that?" Plexi asked. "That was six of the most mastermind criminals," said Flexi. Their names are Bomb Boy, Dr. Grimm, Mrs. Evil, Mr. Key, Saliva Slime Bug, and Ms. Bad.

"Hello, I am Ms. Evil," said Ms. Evil. Then Wonder Girl screamed, "GET OUT NOW!" The villains got mad. "You better take that back or else!" yelled Saliva Slime Bug. "Or else what?" asked Mechanical Med out of curiosity. "We are going to conquer the Universe," all six mastermind villains said together. Then they disappeared without a trace.

"Look on the floor," Plexi said. "At least they left clues," said
Wonder Girl. "Let's get going now," said Flexi. The heroes left in their
super-sized jet.

Their first mission was the Black Hole. It is dangerous, but it is something they have to do. The first three villains were at the Black Hole when they got there.

Bug-a-bites were also there. They are the most ferocious bugs there are. They are larger than the hero's jet. The only way you can destroy that kind of bug is by two acid shoots in the mouth. Flexi had an acid shooter, so that was very hard, and kind of easy. So the Bug-a-bites were destroyed.

Mechanical Med used his tools to help them go through traps, acids, and spikes. Then they finally reached Mrs. Evil, Bomb-Boy and Dr. Grimm. Fighting against them was easy, so they did not have to do much.

Then an amazing thing happened. They found out that they will get a ring for every villain they defeat. The rings are called victory rings and they are very cool.

For the girls, the rings have a rainbow colored pattern inside the heart. The ring for boys is a circle with yellow, blue, orange and green. "This is awesome!" exclaimed Stan Stillman.

The team spent some time together celebrating their accomplish-ments and decided it was time to go on their next mission. "Where do we go next?" asked Flexi. "We go to the Milky Way," said Plexi.

The Milky Way is the most beautiful place in the galaxy. "Why would mastermind villains want to go to the Milky Way?" asked Aqua Blue. "Good question Aqua Blue. It doesn't make sense," replied Stan Stillman. When they got to the Milky Way, it was time for action.

There were two villains there, Mr. Key and Saliva Slime Bug. The mission got harder this time. Mr. Key and Saliva Slime Bug were not easy to destroy. BOOM! POW! THUNK! The villains were winning until Plexi discovered their weaknesses.

Mr. Key's weakness is that when he cannot open a lock he will lose his powers for 500 years. Saliva Slime Bug's weakness is that when he has no slime left in his body, he looses his powers for 2 million years. Plexi had an idea. It was a brilliant one too.

Two seconds later Plexi asked, "Can you open this for me Mr. Key, it is very urgent. My diary key is in here!" So Mr. Key decided to open it for her so he could get her key and find out her weakness.

He zapped the box and it did not work. He did it two or three times. He finally lost his powers on the third try. This means that he will not have powers for 500 years.

Plexi then turned to Saliva Slime Bug. "Can you open my box for me Saliva Slime Bug?" He agreed to it because he has a key to her box. He unlocked it and all of sudden, SPLASH! "Oh no!" exclaimed Saliva Slime Bug.

He was as clean as clouds when there is no rain. This means he will not have powers for 2 million years. "We will get you some day," vowed Mr. Key and Saliva Slime Bug.

The team got their victory rings and left to go on another mission. Their next and final stop is Ms. Bad's lair in Paris, France on planet Zolar.

When the heroes got to planet Zolar, Plexi knew where Ms. Bad's lair was. Her lair was at the Eiffel Tower. Plexi had the solution. All they would have to do is pull the switch in her lab and she will be defeated.

It wasn't easy getting to her lab. She has laser beams, bombs, traps, and spikes everywhere. France is a very odd country. Paris isn't the city of love. It is the city of oddness on planet Zolar.

All of a sudden a big butterfly came. It got bigger and bigger and bigger. It had sharp teeth, red eyes, and very sharp claws. "Ahhhhhhhhhh," screamed the team. "What are we going to do?" asked Wonder Girl. "I know the answer," said Aqua Blue. "All you have to do is inject this antidote into its wings. The question is: Who is going to do it?" "I will," replied Wonder Girl. It wasn't easy but she did it.

Then they went to the laser beams. "Flexi it's your turn," said Plexi. "Okay Sis," said Flexi. FLIP, FLOP, FLEE, she went. When she got to the end, she turned off the laser beams, which triggered a trap. Luckily, they were standing in the wrong spot. With Mechanical Med using his tools, they then pulled the lever to shut down all the traps.

Then they went to the spikes. "Now it's your turn Aqua Blue and Stan Stillman!" said Wonder Girl. Stan Stillman had to freeze the spikes first so Aqua Blue could slide through easily. "I did my job, now it's your turn Aqua Blue," said Stan Stillman.

Aqua Blue needed Stan Stillman because if he steps on a spike in water form, the spike will inject into his foot and turn him into metal. "Thanks Stan Stillman." Aqua Blue said.

He walked over the frozen spikes and when he got there, he shut all of them down. "Wow, this is the easiest thing I've ever been through." said Mechanical Med.

When they got to the main room, Ms. Bad looked like she was waiting for them. Then all of a sudden, BEEP! "She tricked us!" said Stan Stillman. "We already know that!!" yelled Flexi. "Don't you know that we have the smartest alien in the universe?" said Mechanical Med. "I know that. That is why I put a brainwasher on her," said Ms. Bad. "WHAT?" screamed the team.

"I will let her have her brain if you all leave except Plexi and Flexi,"
Ms. Bad said. "You can't do this Flexi," said Wonder Girl. "I accept your
Offer," said Flexi. Then Ms. Bad let everyone go except Plexi and Flexi.
"I'll keep my word," said Ms. Bad.

"What are we going to do?" asked Aqua Blue. "I don't know," responded Wonder girl. "Without Plexi and Flexi we are not much of a team."

In the mean time, in the lab. . . "Do you know why you are here?" asked Ms. Bad. "No," responded Plexi. "Well I have you here because I want to be Queen of Zolar! Ha ha ha ha ha," laughed Ms. Bad. "I don't get it, why?" asked Plexi? "Wow, the smartest girl in the universe doesn't even know that? Don't you twins know you are the Princesses of Zolar and you can get everyone to vote me Queen? If I become Queen, I will rule all of Zolar and after that the Universe. Ha ha ha ha ha," laughed Ms. Bad again.

Mechanical Med used his tools to open the door. Then all of a sudden, ZAP! "Ouuuuuuuuuch!" said Plexi and Flexi together. "STOP!" yelled Aqua Blue. "SPIN!" said Wonder girl and she spun Ms. Bad around.

"FREEZE!" said Stan Sillman and he froze her. Then Aqua Blue finished Ms. Bad off with his slip move. When he releases water, bad guys slip on the water.

"Thank you for helping us catch Ms. Bad and her gang," said the Universe Police. "I think these rings are yours."

"Yes they are," replied the team.

When they put their rings together, it created a rainbow of justice, friendship, and love. "Wow" they all said. They would live in peace until more bad guys come.

THE END or IS IT?